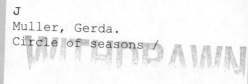
40050

Muller, Gerda
Circle of seasons

WITHDRAWN

Mechanicsburg Public Library

60 South Main Street

Mechanicsburg, Ohio 43044

513-834-2004

DEMCO

CIRCLE *of* SEASONS

CIP Data is available · All rights reserved · First published in the United States 1995 by Dutton Children's Books,
a division of Penguin Books USA Inc. 375 Hudson Street, New York, New York 10014
Originally published in 1994 as four separate titles: *Spring*, *Summer*, *Autumn*, and *Winter*,
by Christofoor Publishers, Zeist, the Netherlands · Text by Lucia Monfried · Design by Semadar Megged
Printed in Hong Kong · First American Edition · ISBN 0-525-45394-6 · 10 9 8 7 6 5 4 3 2 1

CIRCLE OF SEASONS

GERDA MULLER

DUTTON CHILDREN'S BOOKS
NEW YORK

The seasons form a circle that goes around the year.

In spring, the first warm days bring everything bursting forth—green shoots from the ground and frisky baby animals to chase in the sunshine.

Then come the long hot afternoons of summer.

By fall, everything is ready for harvest, and we fill our baskets with earth's bounty.

In winter, our breath makes a frosty mist in the crisp cold air as we grab our sleds for a ride in the snow.

As one season passes, another one arrives.
What special joys will the next season bring?

SPRING

You know it's
spring when . . .

The air feels so warm, and the trees look so green,

and we can prepare the garden for planting.

And we ride out to the farm on
a bright, breezy day to see
the new baby animals—
chicks and a kid,

shiny-eyed bunnies and playful pups.

Everything seems new in spring.

SUMMER

You know it's
summer when . . .

The very best place to be
is the beach, licking
ice-cream cones,

cooling off in the
water, or reading
a good book.

When summer evenings are perfect
for picnic suppers,

and summer afternoons are
perfect for playing.

Everything is so fresh—cherries from the trees and flowers from the garden.

fALL

You know it's
fall when ...

The apples turn ripe, and the air turns brisk,
and the cold rain comes tumbling down.

School is open and beckons us in.

Outdoors the leaves are glorious gold and brown,

and indoors we can make things
with what we have gathered.

We watch the days grow shorter and think
how good it would be to curl up
like a warm, furry puppy.

Winter

You know it's winter when …

It's cold outside, and we bundle up
to skate on the ice

and play in the snow, which has fallen
as fast as the snowballs fly now.

We can make a snowman or
find a tree in the woods,

but we don't forget the birds.

When our toes
are frozen,

we can gather around
Grandfather for a story
by the fire.

And we celebrate our favorite holidays—
Christmas and Hanukkah, joyous days of giving
that light the way to year's end.

The seasons form a circle. The end of the year signals the beginning of a new one, as surely as the first flower will come from under the snow-covered earth.

Welcome, new year! Welcome, spring!